The Dark Blue Bike at No. 17

KT-161-873

Tammy and Jake find out about
friendship and bullying

Catherine Mackenzie

© Catherine Mackenzie 2003
Published by Christian Focus Publications
Geanies House, Fearn, Tain, Ross-shire,
IV20 1TW, Scotland, UK.

Cover illustration by Dave Thompson
Bee Hive Illustration
All other illustrations by Chris Rothero
Bee Hive Illustration.

Printed and bound in Great Britain by Cox and
Wyman, Reading.
ISBN 1-85792-732-X

All rights reserved. No part of this publication may be
reproduced, stored in a retrieval system, or transmitted,
in any form, by any means, electronic, mechanical,
photocopying, recording or otherwise without the
prior permission of the publisher or a licence
permitting restricted copying. In the U.K. such
licences are issued by the Copyright Licensing Agency,
90 Tottenham Court Road, London W1P 9HE
www.christianfocus.com

For Moirs and Shones

~ with thanks and smiles ~

Catherine

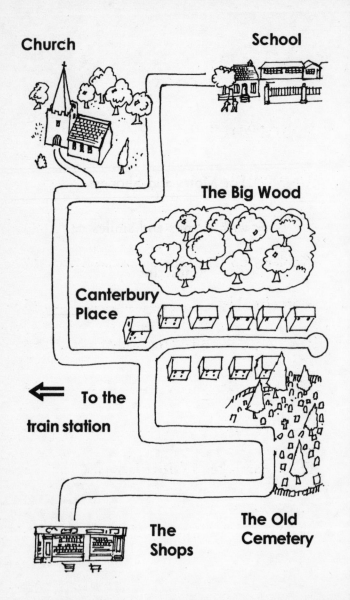

Church

School

The Big Wood

Canterbury
Place

← To the
train station

The Old
Cemetery

The
Shops

Contents

The Dark Blue Bike

The MacDonalds lived at Number 11, Canterbury Place. Jake and Tammy MacDonald thought their house was the best house on the whole street as it had a big back garden with a tall, green, oak tree. Jake was the eldest.

He was eight years old, soon to be nine and Tammy had just turned five.

Jake was secretly hoping for a new bike when he became nine years old. His old bike was a bit rusty and the saddle was torn. Jake's dad had taped it up with some sticky-tape from his D.I.Y. box but Jake couldn't help hoping that when his birthday came mum and dad would buy him a brand new bike. Just like the bike he had seen down at the supermarket this morning.

"It was cool," thought Jake as he remembered the glossy dark blue paint and the shiny metallic fittings. When they had come back out from the supermarket the bike had gone. So Jake didn't see who was riding it.

As they drove out of the supermarket car park Jake suddenly remembered something that made his face fall.

Today was the last day of the summer holidays and tomorrow he would be back to school. He tried to forget about it for the moment and in his head tried to work out why it was that the green Morris Minor was making such a peculiar noise. It wasn't peculiar that the car was making noises - it was just that Jake had never heard the car make this particular noise before. Mrs MacDonald sighed and hit the car on the dash-board, "Come on!" she groaned as the car spluttered up the hill. With a grumble and a groan the car coughed its way up the road - finally grinding its way into the drive way of Number 11.

"We should get a new car!" Tammy, Jake's sister, exclaimed.

Mrs MacDonald sighed, "That would be nice, but it's out of the question. It's just far too expensive. It's all we can do to keep taking this pile of junk to the garage each time!"

Mum slammed the car door a little roughly as she got out. It looked as though she was a bit annoyed with it. Jake ignored the comment about garage bills and went back to day-dreaming about his birthday present.

Once they had all taken off their coats and hung them on the rail Mum gave Tammy and Jake household chores to do. Jake emptied some of the shopping bags and put stuff away. Tammy was given the job of putting the fruit in the fruit bowl and filling Doggers water dish. He was feeling a bit thirsty and his tongue was flopping out of his mouth - doggy drool dripping on the lino.

Mum was busy chattering away about the things that were going to be happening over the next few days.

"Oh bother! I quite forgot! It's Emma's birthday on Friday!"

"Who is Emma?" Jake asked.

"My old school friend - we always send birthday cards to each other. We've done it since we were twelve years old. She was my best friend at school - we were really close. I never had a sister - but Emma was just like a sister to me. We used to tell each other everything! Well... let's see... there's a card in this drawer somewhere." Mum rooted around in the drawer until she brought out a card with Happy Birthday written on it in bright letters, "Emma will love this. I'll just write it and then one of you can go to the postbox for me. I can't believe that the last time I saw her was over twenty years ago." Mum sounded a little wistful and sad as she spoke about her old school friend.

All of a sudden the doorbell rang and Jake went to answer it. It was a few of the boys from the street who wanted to get a football game going. So Jake grabbed his boots from underneath the kitchen table and ran out to join his friends. He couldn't imagine life without them, Dave, Robert, Mark and Timothy.

But straight away Jake noticed that not all of the usual gang were there - "Where's Timothy?" Jake asked.

Dave stopped mid-stride and looked at Jake astonished. "Haven't you heard? Tim's dad's been offered a job up North. They've had to move. It was just last week. I suppose you never heard about it because you've all been away at your gran's house."

Jake stopped and stared at Dave.

He couldn't believe it. Timothy had sat beside him in class all of last year. They had gotten on really well. Timothy was one of Jake's best friends.

Dave saw how upset Jake was looking. "I'm sure he would liked to have said goodbye but they had to move quickly. Maybe the teacher at school can give you his address and you can write to him."

But Jake wasn't that sure. Surely if Tim had been a real friend he would have said goodbye? If Tim had really liked him he'd have left a note or something. Jake kicked at some mud with his football boot. He didn't care. Who wanted Timothy Green as a friend anyway - not him that was for sure!

As they all got ready to head home after the game Jake noticed that one or two of the older boys had received bikes for their birthdays. But there was no sign of the dark blue bike. In one way Jake was glad - he would have felt really jealous of the boy who had that bike. It was good that it didn't belong to a friend of his.

However, when Dad took him and Tammy out to get a pizza that night Jake spotted the dark blue bike propped up against the window outside the pizza parlour.

He really, really, wanted one.

"Dad," Jake said quietly, "Do you see that blue mountain bike over there?"

Dad looked, and whistled. "Wow, Jake. That's a beauty isn't it? Perhaps you can save up for one after you've got these new soccer trainers you want. You might be able to get one like that second hand eventually. But brand new, it would cost you three hundred pounds at least!" Jake sighed. No bike for his birthday then. Dad continued, "Mum was wondering if you'd like us to give you money towards the new trainers you want for your birthday?"

Jake quietly said, "Yes Dad, that's great," as his Dad got out of the car to get their pizzas. But Jake felt really disappointed. He should have known his parents could never afford a bike like that. Jake knew how hard Mum and Dad worked and how difficult it was sometimes to pay all the bills. But Jake just couldn't get the thought of the beautiful, blue, shiny, bike out of his head. "I'd do almost anything to get a bike like that," thought Jake.

"Tammy," Jake asked, "What do you want most of all in the whole world?"

Tammy thought, long and hard while chewing the end of one of her blonde pig-tails. "I want to go to school," was her decision.

Jake sighed. Typical. Tammy had been speaking about nothing else for weeks. She was desperate to go to school. Tomorrow she would be lucky as it was her first day, and she couldn't wait.

The First Day Back

The next morning Tammy was really excited. "I can't wait. I can't wait," she kept saying to herself, jumping up and down on the spot. Dad smiled and said jokingly, "You'll just have to my love. If I can't get this sweat shirt on you, you won't be going anywhere."

Tammy stood still but her eyes were shining and her teeth were sparkling as she grinned from ear to ear. "I'm starting school today!" she gasped.

"Yes, we know," Mum said, sighing. "That's the twentieth time you've said it and you haven't had breakfast yet. Now be careful I don't want you spilling milk all down your front."

Tammy smiled. She was all smiles today because this was her very first day at school and she had been looking forward to it for weeks. She had a new white blouse and a navy blue skirt and a sweat shirt with a special badge.

Tammy noticed that her mum had sewn her name onto all her clothes. Though she was sure she would never lose them. But Mum was prepared for anything. The first day of the new school term was a very important day for the MacDonalds.

"Everyone ready for breakfast then?" asked Dad. "Jake are you ready?" he asked anxiously.

"Yes Dad," Jake sighed from the top of the stairs. He was trying to sort his tie in the mirror and finding it a bit tricky. Tammy didn't have to wear a tie but all the older pupils did. Jake wore a white shirt which felt a bit uncomfortable after wearing T-shirts and jeans all summer. Dad grinned, "It's been a few weeks since you've had to wear that old thing. You're out of practice, let me help."

Jake turned round and let his Dad sort his tie for him. He could see Tammy, jumping up and down again in the hallway. Mum was switching on the toaster and placing some bacon under the grill. Jake's tummy rumbled. Bacon and ketchup toasted sandwiches were a real treat for breakfast. Dad gave Jake a hug and patted him on the back.

"Go and get it then. Nothing like a good breakfast to set you up for the day."

Jake wondered why parents always said that. Perhaps it was because it was true? And when it was toasted bacon sandwiches for breakfast Jake didn't disagree. The smell of the bacon, just beginning to cook, pricked his nostrils. Jake was hungry.

As he tucked into the delicious crispy bacon he sighed again. Tammy was still as high as a kite. He could understand that she was excited about the new school but did she have to go

on and on about it? Jake wasn't looking
forward to it at all. He wasn't going to
get the blue bike for his birthday and
he was also going to miss Timothy.
He had hoped there might have been
a card from Timothy this morning - just
to say good luck and by the way guess
where I'm living. But there wasn't.

Normally Jake loved the first day of
the new term. It was good to meet up
with friends you hadn't seen all
summer, finding out everyone's news
and opening your new books and
jotters, ready for work. But this year it
was different. This year Jake's best

friend, Timothy, wouldn't be there.

Timothy had helped Jake with spelling and Jake had helped Timothy with maths. They had been good friends. But Jake shook his head. Timothy wasn't his friend anymore and that was that.

After breakfast Jake and Tammy helped Mum tidy up. Tammy dried some cutlery while Mum dried the plates. Jake took the rubbish out and when he came back in, Mum was putting away the last of the cups.

"It's time for family prayers now," she said and Tammy ran through to the TV room for the Bible. She took it back into the kitchen where they all sat down ready to listen to what mum was going to read. She leafed through the pages and stopped at a story about a man called Nehemiah. He had been a special servant to a foreign king long, long ago. He had been taken away from his real country as a prisoner, but things had gone well for him and he became a trusted and respected member of the foreign king's workers.

"But one day," Mum told them, "Nehemiah had some bad news. He had heard that the people who were trying to rebuild the capital city of his country were having problems. The city was called Jerusalem, and Nehemiah loved it. The people in it were special to God and God even had a special building there, called the temple. But when the country was defeated in battle, Jerusalem had been destroyed. Nehemiah really wanted his home to be rebuilt. He hated to think of the walls broken down and the gates smashed to pieces. He wondered what he should do. He wanted to go home but he was frightened to ask the King."

"Why was that Mum?" Tammy asked.

"Well, the King was very powerful and might have stopped Nehemiah. I think Nehemiah was scared that the King would be angry and not allow him to leave. So what did he do? Did he try to escape?"

Jake thought a bit.

"No he didn't," said Mum. "Did he go up to the King and demand to be sent home? He didn't do that either. Instead he prayed to God. When Nehemiah went in to see the King, the King saw how anxious Nehemiah looked and immediately asked what the matter was. Here was Nehemiah's chance.

Quickly he prayed again. This time it was a really short prayer, 'Lord help me.' Then he asked the King if he could go home to help rebuild the city of Jerusalem. The King said, 'Yes.' God had answered Nehemiah's prayers."

Dad smiled as mum finished the story and closed the Bible once again. "You see God is always listening. When we cry to him for help he is there to hear and answer us. Even when you are in school and you need to pray to God you can do it quickly and quietly. God will hear you just the same as if you were praying at church or at home. Sometimes I pray in the car."

"You don't close your eyes though Dad do you?" asked Tammy anxiously.

"No Tammy, I don't," laughed Dad. "That would be too dangerous. You don't have to close your eyes to pray, or stand up or kneel. You can pray to God at any time, anywhere. So let's pray now."

Dad cleared his throat and began to speak to God, "Dear God, we are so glad that you are here with us, listening to us. Tammy and Jake are starting school today.

It's Tammy's first day and she is really excited. Jake is going back to school to a new class and new lessons. So we ask for you to protect Tammy and Jake and to help them. Thank you God for how you love us and protect us. We are sorry for our sins. Please help us to be better and to love you more.

As Mum is staring her new job at

the health centre, we ask you to look after her and help her too.

Thank you for your Son Jesus Christ who died for us on the cross. We ask all these things in Jesus name, Amen."

Tammy, Jake and Mum said Amen too and then Mum looked at the clock. "Right, everybody, quick march. Jake get your bag. Tammy, your bag is here by the fridge. Here are your packed lunches. There's a snack in there too for break time."

Jake came back into the kitchen and stuffed his packed lunch inside his bag. Dad gave Tammy a kiss and a cuddle and was about to ruffle Jake's hair when Mum squeeled, "Don't. He's just combed that!" Instead he gave Jake a big bear hug. As they all got in the car Dad stood to wave them off. Jake laughed as Dad pulled a funny face and he pulled one back.

Perhaps the day would go alright after all... even though Timothy couldn't be bothered to write and hadn't bothered to tell his best friend he was moving away.

As Mum turned round the corner of Canterbury Place, Jake turned round to see Number 11 disappear slowly.

Tammy was singing for the twenty-first time that morning, "I'm staaaaarting schoool. I'm staaaarting schoooool!"

As Tammy sang on about what a great thing it was to be going to school Jake sighed again. A bit of peace and quiet would be nice.

"Not so loud Tammy," Jake and his mum said at the same time. Everyone laughed.

Problems on Day One

The traffic had been busy that morning, especially as they drew near to the school. So Jake made sure that he took hold of Tammy's hand as she got out of the car. Mum hurried them along towards the year one classrooms where Mum took Tammy into the class to meet her school teacher.

Mum's new job started this morning too and she was just as excited as Tammy.

Mum was going to be working part-time at the local health centre. "It's mornings only for the first while so I'll be back when you return from school," Mrs MacDonald smiled.

Dad worked too and had recently changed his job and was now working at the academy across town. It was the school that Jake would be going to in a few years time.

Tammy's teacher showed Tammy where to hang her coat and where the play corner and the crayons were. Tammy, who had been feeling a little nervous for the first time that day, smiled when she saw the play corner and immediately went to join some other little girls who were playing with some pretend saucepans.

Mum smiled and called out to her "Remember, Mrs Thompson will pick you up after lunch. I will be home soon after that."

Jake waved goodbye to Mum as the little Morris Minor car headed,

 spluttering, out the school gate. Jake was sure that Mum must be nervous. It was a new start for everyone.

It was arithmetic first thing and Jake was good at sums. But spelling was after that... and Jake wasn't good at spelling. Timothy had always helped Jake with his spellings. "But who needs Timothy anyway," Jake sulked.

Jake did all his sums correctly and then mis-spelt all his words.

His teacher wasn't pleased. "You've

forgotten a lot over the summer, Jake. You will have to do extra home-work."

Jake sighed. It was all Timothy's fault - if he had been here it wouldn't have happened. Then at break time the whole class charged out to play. Jake's class mates were soon running round the school yard playing games or chasing each other. Jake felt a bit out of it. Nobody had asked him to play. The boys he usually played football with were playing with some of the older kids and they didn't need any more players on their team. Jake remembered what it used to be like at break time if there wasn't a football match on. Jake and Timothy would pretend to be explorers or something. Jake wondered if Timothy was playing games with some other children in another school somewhere.

"He probably doesn't miss me at all," Jake frowned.

Jake noticed that Tammy was making lots of friends. The junior classes had a playground to themselves and they were all playing games with their teachers or making castles and things in the sand pit.

Tammy was with two other little girls

and they were all holding hands. For a moment Jake felt jealous of Tammy. He wished he had some friends.

Jake wandered off to the other side of the playground and waited until the bell rang again. He felt miserable.

When the school bell rang, Jake went back to class. In the corner of his eye was a little tear. It just wasn't fair. Why did Timothy's dad have to get a job in another town? Why?

Jake felt so horrible that he decided he wouldn't even go to school the next day. Jake was going to do something really silly. He was going to skip school and not tell anyone. Jake thought and thought about this plan all afternoon.

He didn't think that his teacher might wonder where he was and ask his mum.

He didn't think that his mum would worry when she heard and he didn't think that someone would see him hiding behind the hedge just as everyone was about to go into school the next morning. But that was exactly what happened. Daniel Conner spotted Jake and it meant that Jake was in a lot of trouble.

More trouble

Jake, couldn't believe that he had been spotted. Daniel Conner had run in the school gates at the last minute. He was always late. He was one of those kids who was always last, always in trouble and always getting other people into trouble too. But just as he stumbled in the school gates he stopped to tie his shoe lace and spotted Jake, hiding behind the hedge.

Jake hadn't really thought about what he was going to do that day. But when Daniel spotted him a chilly feeling spread down his spine. Would Daniel ignore him and move on? Not likely, Daniel had a reputation for being bad tempered and scary. He was the same age as Jake but was in the other class. Sometimes when Jake and Daniel's classes joined together for sports or assembly Jake noticed the mean way Daniel treated one or two of the other kids. He poked fun at the teachers if they were reading a Bible story - but he was always careful to do it when they weren't looking.

Jake looked straight into the eyes of Daniel and something told him that he was really in trouble now.

"What are you doing there you little wimp!" sneered Daniel. Jake jumped. "What's a little goody-goody like you doing skipping school? Wait till I tell the teachers about you," Daniel spat at Jake and kicked some dust in his face. "I've seen you going to church - think you're better than me do you?

We'll see..." With that Daniel disappeared through the big school doors laughing. Jake stood there, frightened, unsure about what to do. Then he was spotted by a teacher.

"Come on then Jake, don't dilly-dally. Get to class. Your teacher is waiting."

Jake sighed picked up his bag and went to class. His teacher told him to stay behind after school to clean the classroom as punishment for being late. Then Jake spent all morning hoping that Daniel wouldn't tell the teachers about what he had been doing. During break Jake watched the other children play on the swings and kick the football around, but he didn't join in. Daniel was pointing in his direction and the scary feeling shivered down Jake's back again. When the school bell rang and all the children disappeared to class Jake made a quick dash to the toilets. He'd been

frightened to go there while Daniel was still around. Jake had heard that Daniel and his friends liked to pounce on people in the toilets when the teachers weren't looking. Jake thought that Daniel would now be on his way to class so he ran to the toilets to freshen up. If he was quick about it he wouldn't be late. There was a water fountain there where you could get a drink from and Jake was very thirsty. As Jake bent over it - a hand shoved him in the back and Jake's face was held underneath the water. Jake coughed and spluttered and tried to get his breath and then the hand disappeared. Jake heard voices laughing and shouting as the doors of the boys toilets swung shut. Suddenly the doors swung open again very quickly. Daniel stood there laughing. "I wouldn't bother telling your precious little teacher about this ... wouldn't want her to know what you're really like now would you..."

Jake sniffed, he wasn't going to cry in front of Daniel. But why did he feel as if this was all his fault. He was sure it wasn't... but then he had been planning to skip school. Daniel knew all about that.

Daniel slammed the door shut again and Jake heard him shouting out as he swaggered down the corridor, "Think you're better than me? We'll see..."

Jake spent the next two minutes crying on his own in the toilets. But the sound of a teacher's voice in the distance made him jump again. If he was late for another class he'd really be in trouble. He wished he could speak to Timothy ... but Timothy was no longer there and Jake felt as though he didn't have a friend in the world. Perhaps he didn't deserve to have friends... perhaps he would never have a good friend like Timothy ever again.

That afternoon Jake's class had a science project. It was really interesting and Jake learned lots about plants and how they grow.

Later on Jake enjoyed helping his teacher clean up the classroom. She gave him a duster to brush off all the chalk writing from the board. Then she asked him to sharpen the pencils. Jake did a very good job and she was pleased.

Then as Jake was pulling on his coat the teacher suggested that he might like to take one of the new science books home for a read.

"I noticed what a good job you did on the project. You can borrow the book and give it back to me tomorrow. But take care of it. We've only got a few."

Jake grinned from ear to ear. He couldn't wait to have a good read of the book when he got home. Perhaps Timothy would write him a letter too. There might be one waiting for Jake when he got home. Jake grabbed his bag and ran out the school gates as fast as he could.

He decided to go home by walking through the woods at the back of Canterbury place. It was always interesting walking through the woods as there were lots of birds and sometimes a squirrel or two to spot.

He hadn't been in the woods for very long when he heard a rustling to his left. He looked over and saw Daniel climbing over the fence of Number 17. Another boy in a black shirt followed him. The other boy was laughing ... "There's the little rat we drowned at lunch time. Let's get him Daniel."

Jake tried to back away, but tripped over a tree root. He had forgotten that Daniel had moved to Canterbury Place. Just as Jake had thought that things couldn't get worse he realised that Daniel was now his neighbour.

Daniel and the other boy drew up alongside Jake - Daniel stood in front of Jake and the other boy stood behind him. Daniel pushed first and then the other boy. Jake was shoved around and then kicked on the shin.

"Teacher's pet, teacher's pet," Daniel sneered. "You must love your little teacher very much to help her out so much. Little Jake is being such a good little boy." Every word Daniel said sounded as if it was pure hatred.

Then Daniel reached inside Jake's school bag and took out all his books and threw them into a puddle.

"Don't do that Daniel!" Jake yelled.

"I'll do what I like," laughed Daniel. Picking up Jake's books he dropped them on the ground one by one and then stood on them - even the brand new science book. Jake just sat at the edge of the puddle and cried. Before Daniel climbed the fence again he yelled across the wood, "If you tell I will tell on you! Your mum will be furious and then everyone in that pokey little church of yours will know what a really bad boy you are." Daniel laughed even more as his head disappeared over the fence.

58

Jake reached down to pick up the science book and tried to brush the worst of the dirt off it with the sleeve of his jacket. When Jake got home Mrs Macdonald was in the kitchen so Jake tiptoed up the stairs to his room and laid the books out on the desk. He would try and clean them up with a damp towel. Then Mum called that tea was ready. Taking a deep breath Jake left the books and tried to act as if nothing had happened. Although it was time for tea Jake didn't feel like eating anything. He felt awful. And he'd been wrong about the second post. There had been no letters from anyone.

"Were you expecting a letter Jake?" Mum asked, puzzled.

Jake shrugged his shoulders. "Maybe."

Mum looked surprised. "You never send any letters Jake - that's why you don't get any."

That was true... but Jake thought it was up to Timothy to write first. After all it was Timothy who had moved away without saying anything. "Why should I have to write a letter first," Jake thought angrily.

Jake was quiet all through tea. He

didn't even feel like watching television afterwards. Mum asked, "Is there anything the matter?"

Jake just shook his head and mumbled something about his homework. Tammy showed Jake her new story book for the eighth time since he had got home. Gruffly, Jake told Tammy to take her book away. And he stormed off up to his room.

After Mum had soothed Tammy's tears, she came up to speak to him. That was when she noticed his books on the desk. The dirt was still smudged on the paper and the corners were all bent.

"Jake! What happened?"

Jake didn't say anything, but he looked worried. If he told Mum about Daniel then Daniel would tell. Jake was too frightened to do anything.

"Did you drop them in a puddle or something?" Jake's mum asked.

Jake nodded. "Do you think my new science book will be alright?" he asked anxiously. Mum opened the cover and gave it a quick dust. "Yes, it will be alright. Thankfully it's got one of those wipe clean covers so the mud won't stick... and the corners aren't bent like these other ones. What were you doing?" Jake knew that his mum was suspicious and was thankful that she didn't ask any more questions. She just took the books downstairs to see if she could clean them up.

Jake buried his head in his pillow. He was hiding things from everybody... teachers, his family, Mum. Things just kept getting worse. All he had wanted to do was skip school. Now because he had done one wrong thing he kept doing other wrong things. One thing just led to another. Jake remembered the time he had broken mum's vase and lied about it to her. He had blamed it on the dog. But eventually he had said sorry about that. He had told his mum and then he had asked Jesus to become his friend.

A thought hit Jake suddenly, out of the blue, "You should speak to God about this." Jake wondered, perhaps God would stop Daniel from bullying him.

Jake closed his eyes and prayed. "God help me. Daniel is being really horrible to me and I am really scared."

As he opened his eyes Jake felt a little better. His prayer hadn't been very long but he had meant every word he said. Then Jake remembered the story about Nehemiah and how he had asked God to help him. Perhaps God would now help Jake but Jake wasn't very sure.

The Dark Blue Bike Discovery

The following morning Jake and Tammy had cereal and toast and a glass of orange juice for breakfast. You didn't get toasted bacon sandwiches every morning at Number 11. But that made them more special when you did have them. So Jake didn't mind.

As Tammy and Jake scraped their bowls and drank their last drops of orange juice. Dad brought the Bible out again and they all sat back to listen to a story.

"Remember Nehemiah," said Dad. "Well he got to Jerusalem and the city walls were rebuilt. But there were problems. The builders had to build but they had to be ready to fight too. There were people who wanted to kill Nehemiah to stop him building the walls. They wanted to spoil it all."

Mum added, "These people were bullies, right?"

Dad nodded, "Yes, that's a good way to describe them. But God helped Nehemiah here too. His enemies tried to frighten him, they said nasty things to him and even planned to attack the city and cause lots of trouble. But then Nehemiah and the people prayed to God. They also set guards on the city to keep watch. Nehemiah reminded everyone that God would fight for them. Fifty-two days later the wall was rebuilt."

"That wasn't too long," said Jake.

"No," agreed Dad. "They worked very hard. And after it was all finished the people of Israel all said sorry to God for the wrong things they had done and asked him to forgive them. They promised to obey him in the future too."

"Yes," said Mum. "They asked God for help, he helped them and then they remembered the bad things they'd done and they said sorry for them, but they also said they wouldn't do them again. Nehemiah, prayed and trusted in God, but he also set guards on the city to keep watch. He worked very hard on the wall. Nehemiah wasn't stupid and he wasn't lazy. We must always trust in God, but God has also given us arms and legs and voices and brains. We should use them."

As Jake picked up his books again to go to school, (Mum had managed to clean them quite well) he thought about the story of this man called Nehemiah. Jake had asked for help. Perhaps God would give it to him too? But Jake also realised that he had to say sorry to God for the wrong things that he had done. Jake knew he had been wrong to try and stay away from school and that he had been wrong to lie to his mum. But Jake wasn't sure about how God would help him. Jake wasn't sure what he was supposed to do either. Nehemiah set guards on the city and built a wall. But what was Jake supposed to do?

This whole thing made him feel awful. He was scared of Daniel and he wasn't sure if God could do anything about him.

"Well, how about walking to school today Jake ... there's plenty of time this morning," Dad looked at Jake who was hanging around the kitchen not doing very much. Jake felt his stomach lurch. Walking to school would mean walking past Daniel's house. What if Daniel came out and started bullying him. Jake shivered. "It's too cold Dad, can't I get a lift?"

Dad looked surprised, Jake didn't normally complain of the cold. In fact he was usually outside playing in all weathers. "That's not like you Jake?" Dad said.

"Please Dad, I don't want to walk to school. Really... it looks like rain and Mum's going that way anyway..."

"Oh alright then Jake," Mum said with a sigh. "But I don't know what's gotten into you lately. Dropping books in puddles and being too lazy to walk to school in the mornings." Jake tried to argue but Mum wasn't having it. "Yes Jake I think it's just laziness. You can get a lift today but from now on you'll have to walk to school as usual - and Tammy can go with you."

That made Jake really scared. If Tammy was with him would Daniel hurt her too? This was getting very serious.

When Mum dropped them both off at school Jake was relieved that there was no sign of Daniel. Daniel never, ever, came to school early.

Jake avoided Daniel in the playground too. When he spotted him in the distance he hid behind some rubbish bins. Jake didn't even go to the toilets on his own - he always made sure that there was a teacher in the corridor nearby or another pupil within shouting distance. However, just when Jake thought he had found a nice quiet spot to eat his packed lunch Daniel and his friends pounced on him - grabbed his lunch and left him with nothing but an old apple core.

Jake hid behind the dustbins until the bell went. Then he ran into the classroom so fast that his teacher gasped, "You are not a hurricane Jake. Slow down!"

How come teachers always managed to have something smart to say?

The following day was just as bad - if not worse - Daniel and his friends kept following Jake round the school whispering about him. In sports Daniel deliberately tripped Jake up when the teacher wasn't looking and when the boys went into the changing rooms Jake discovered that someone had left his clothes in the shower and they were now soaked through. A teacher gave him a change of clothing... but everyone sniggered at Jake for the rest of the afternoon.

Jake realised that if it had been someone else he would have been laughing at them too - so he promised that in the future he wouldn't join in with the crowd when they laughed and made fun of someone like this. Jake hated the way that Daniel deliberately followed him around laughing at him and calling him names. The punches and shoves made him cry... and so did the names and the nasty comments. Tears would trickle out of his eyes and sobs catch at the back of his throat. Why was God letting all these horrible things happen?

The only thing that was keeping Jake going was the thought that now there was a whole weekend stretched out in front of him. No school, no spellings, no Daniel. Jake almost felt good. But he would have felt better if Timothy was here. Jake remembered the great football games they used to have at the weekends. As he wandered home Jake wished for the one hundredth time that Timothy hadn't left. He thought about asking the teacher for Timothy's address. But Jake thought, "If Timothy doesn't want to speak to me, I don't want to speak to him."

Thinking this didn't make Jake feel better, it made him feel grumpier.

As Jake walked home that afternoon he still kept an eye out for Daniel but didn't see him anywhere. To make sure Daniel didn't throw his books in a puddle like he did the other day Jake walked the long way home and not through the woods. Daniel wouldn't dare hurt him in the middle of the street. So that was why Jake was walking past Daniel Connor's front door and that was how he spotted the shiny blue bike. He couldn't believe it. Jake hadn't thought about the blue bike for

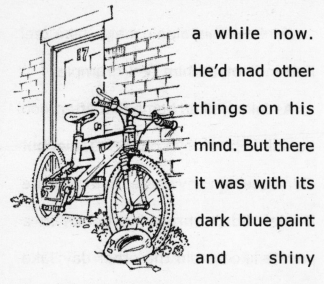

a while now. He'd had other things on his mind. But there it was with its dark blue paint and shiny chrome fittings, and it was outside Daniel's house.

What was it doing there? Then Jake worked it out. "This must be Daniel's bike!"

The old longings resurfaced. Jake was desperate for a new bike. He wanted a new bike just like Daniel's.

He looked and looked at it and didn't seem to care that Daniel might look out of the house at any minute and spot him standing there.

But then Jake noticed that Daniel's dad's car wasn't there. The house was dark and no one was around. Daniel's dog wasn't even there, as it usually was, barking in the back garden.

A neighbour shouted across to Jake. "Are you looking for Daniel?"

Jake nodded, it wasn't exactly untrue, but it wasn't exactly true either.

"He and his dad always go to London

at the weekends you know. They won't be back until Monday now."

Jake nodded. He had wondered how he had never seen Daniel playing in the park at weekends or out with his football. As the old man disappeared Jake wandered over to the shiny blue bike. He let his hand feel the beautiful shimmering chrome and he let out a low whistle as he saw all the gears.

"This is an expensive bike," gasped Jake. "Dad was right. He and Mum could never afford one as good as this... and it's Daniel's."

Something inside Jake made him feel

really angry and jealous. How could Daniel's mum and dad afford a bike as good as this? It wasn't fair. Jake's mum and Dad couldn't afford to get Jake a new bike. Jake was having to save up all his pocket money just so as he could get some new trainers for soccer practice. But here was Daniel, a horrible bully, with a brand new bike.

Jake then grabbed hold of the bike and pushed it out the drive, down the road and round the corner. Running with the bike he went down one street then another until he got to the gates that took you into the woodland. Jake was so angry that he had decided to dump Daniel's brand new bike in the pond, where it would get all dirty and rusty and then be no use anymore.

Jake pushed the bike over tree roots and through muddy puddles and then just as he was about to shove the bike into the dirty, muddy pond a voice shouted at him from behind.

"Jake, what are you doing?"

Jake looked round and saw Dave Johnson from Number 12 staring at him.

Dave was a year older and in the school football team. Jake looked down at his feet and didn't say anything.

"That's Daniel's bike isn't it? I saw him out on it this morning." Jake nodded. "What are you doing pushing it into the pond?"

Jake shrugged his shoulders and then he started to cry. Dave sighed and then he offered Jake his handkerchief. "My mum always makes me have one of these. You can use it if you want. Do you want to tell me what's wrong?"

Jake nodded and told Dave

everything. He told him about Daniel finding him behind the hedge, about Daniel threatening to tell his mum and the teachers and about how Daniel had punched him and thrown all his books into a puddle.

"When I saw his bike I felt so angry. I wanted to get back at him. I know it's wrong Dave."

"Yes, I know you do so it's a good thing I spotted you and stopped you from doing something silly. But I think you've got a bit of a problem. You should tell your mum about it.

Whenever anyone is bullying you you should always tell a parent or a teacher. It's really important."

"I spoke to God about it."

"Well that's good. I know that God helps us when we ask him."

Jake smiled. Dave went to the same church as he did. It was good to have someone about the same age as him going to church.

"But God would want you to tell your mum and to be honest with her too. Tell your parents about what has happened. They will be able to help you. You could also tell a teacher. But you have to tell somebody. You have to tell an adult."

Jake nodded. He had been lying to his mum which was wrong and that was something he had to stop right now. He wasn't sure how he was going to tell her about what had happened but now Jake felt that perhaps this was the other thing he was supposed to do. Like Nehemiah had put guards on the city and worked hard on building the wall, Jake should tell his mum and dad exactly what had happened. That was very important, Jake realised.

Dave took an old rag out of his coat

pocket. He seemed to carry hundreds of things in his pockets. He always had just the right thing to clean a bike or to unblock a pencil sharpener. This time he cleaned up Daniel's bike before he remembered a story he had heard about bullies.

"My uncle told me once that bullies are sometimes bullies because something bad has happened in their lives. We don't see much of Daniel in the park. He's always away at weekends. I wonder if everything is alright? You never see his mum you know."

Jake nodded. Now that he thought about it, he had never seen Daniel's mum, not even once.

Dave continued, "Well my uncle, takes a Sunday school in a church near where my gran lives. One day we went on holiday there. I remember I was having trouble with bullies at that time." Jake looked surprised. "It was at my old school. Two boys were being really nasty to me. Well my uncle told this story about some bullies in the Bible and how Jesus changed them. Zacchaeus was a bully and a thief. He was always stealing peoples' money.

But Jesus went to his house for tea and then Zacchaeus changed. He was no longer a bully and actually helped people instead.

"Then one day the disciples didn't want the kids disturbing Jesus so they roughly told them and their mums to go away. Jesus told them to stop doing that because he loved children. He said that children should come to God if they want to and that nobody should stop them. So I suppose Jesus stood up to bullies but he also helped people, like Zacchaeus, to stop being bullies."

Dave then agreed to take Daniel's

bike back to Number 17 and perhaps give it a bit of a wash.

"He shouldn't have left it outside the house like that. But perhaps he had to leave in a bit of a rush or something? I'll take it back and make sure that it's put out of sight. That way no one is going to steal it or anything."

Jake thanked Dave for helping him and nipped home through the woods and in through the back garden gate of Number 11.

He wondered whether God would help him, but he also wondered whether God would help Daniel to stop being a bully.

Then Jake remembered that he had to speak to his mum. He was going to tell her all that had happened. But before he went in to speak to his mum Jake realised that there was something else he had to do before he even spoke to his mum.

Jake spoke to God and said that he was sorry.

Tammy is a Help

When Jake came in and dumped his school bag in the corner he saw that mum was on the phone. "Who is she speaking to?" Jake asked Tammy.

"I'm not certain, but it's about a boy called Daniel."

"What?" Jake said, astonished.

"Well I've been listening in and I think that someone called Mr Conner has got a boy called Daniel and Daniel's mum is in hospital... far away... and she is very sick. Something horrible is happening because Mum keeps saying, "Oh no," and "Oh dear," and then she's asked if she can help."

Jake was amazed at how much Tammy had heard of the conversation. For a five year old she was very good at eavesdropping.

When Mum came off the phone she asked Jake to make her a cup of tea. "I've got some bad news for you dear,"

 she said. "Do you know Daniel at Number 17?" Jake nodded. "Well, I should have gone round or something. I feel so bad now, but things have been so busy with the new job. Anyway, I've just heard that Daniel's mum has been in hospital for the last six weeks. She is seriously ill in a hospital in London and the only time Daniel and Mr Conner can see her is at weekends.

"Mr Conner has just phoned Joyce at church and asked her if she could look after Daniel for a few days next

96

week while he stays in London with his wife.

Daniel will be coming back tomorrow afternoon on the train and Joyce has asked me if we would mind picking him up and taking him back to hers. She has to work until three o'clock on Saturdays and can't get time off to meet the train. Apparently Daniel is very upset. I think his mum is getting worse instead of better and he doesn't want to leave her behind in London. But his Dad thinks it's for the best so I suppose it is. Do you know him well Jake?"

Jake didn't know what to say about that. He just shrugged his shoulders. "I suppose I know him kind of well," he mumbled. Jake's mum looked at the clock and then quickly drank up her tea. "Right, that's the lasagne nearly done. I'll just put some carrots on the boil and make a salad for tea."

After everyone had finished their meal and the dishes were all washed and dried Mrs MacDonald started to get ready to go out. "I've got a meeting at church. I won't be back until late. So I'll see you both tomorrow." With that she gave Jake and Tammy a kiss and waved as she went out the door. Later on that evening Tammy was packed off to bed by Dad and was given the grand total of three bedtime stories.

Jake felt strange. He had hoped that he would be able to speak to mum about Daniel tonight. He had forgotten all about her meeting at church. He wondered if he should tell Dad. But it just seemed all wrong to be telling them that Daniel was a bully when Daniel's mum was in hospital and Daniel was so upset. Jake didn't know how he felt about Daniel now. He was still scared of him. He still didn't like him. But he was sad for him too.

That night he tossed and turned in his bed. He was glad when it was morning. Saturday morning was always the best. Getting up out of bed he watched some television and then got washed and dressed and went out to play football in the park.

He met Dave there who asked him what his mum had said.

"I haven't told her yet. Something's happened. Daniel's mum is in hospital and I just don't feel right telling mum about Daniel's bullying when things are going so wrong for him. It would make me sound like a tell-tale too."

Dave thought and then he said, "It doesn't matter what has happened. You have to tell someone. It's not telling tales, it's telling the truth."

Jake nodded. He knew Dave was right. "I'll tell mum after we drop Daniel off at Joyce's."

"He's staying at Joyce's?"

"Yes."

"How does he know her?"

"I don't know," Jake said.

A couple of hours later after the third game of football Jake looked at his watch and waved to Dave to say he was off home. Then after lunch mum told Jake to get his coat. "We're off to pick up Daniel now," she said.

"I'm coming too. I'm coming to pick up Daniel," chirped Tammy.

So all three of them and Dogger clambered into the car. Dogger barked excitedly as Mum carefully drove Dad's blue fiesta car out of the drive way. Mum thought that driving the Morris Minor on such an important errand was taking too much of a risk.

"It's got a mind of it's own that car!" she'd say each morning as she tried to get it to start.

As they waited at the station Mum sighed as the announcer spoke over the loud speaker. "The 3 o'clock train from London, Euston, has been delayed due to an electrical fault. It is now due at 3.35."

"Oh bother!" said Mum. "We'll have to wait. You two stay in the car with Dogger. I'll go and get us all some sweets from the newsagents. I won't be a minute."

Jake sighed, he wondered when he was ever going to get a chance to speak to his mum. He wasn't looking forward to sharing a car with Daniel either. He hoped Daniel didn't tell his mum about the hedge incident before he did.

Mum returned to the car with the sweets and a steaming cup of tea that she'd got from the hot drinks counter. After Tammy and Jake had had a mouthful Mum finished the cup and put it in the bin. Then she went to check with the station master about the time of the delayed train. Tammy watched mum cross the car park. Then she asked Jake a question.

"Do you like Daniel?"

Jake stopped and looked at her.

"What do you mean?"

"Is he a nice boy?" she asked.

Jake looked at Tammy and sighed. This time he was going to tell the truth.

"Not really," he said quietly. "He's actually quite nasty to me at school."

Tammy looked surprised and worried

and curious all at the same time.

"What happened?"

"He saw me do something bad and he says he will tell Mum, if I tell her that he has been pushing me about and throwing my books in puddles."

Tammy gasped, "It was Daniel who threw your books in a puddle?"

"Yes, but don't tell Mum. Because I'm going to tell her myself. It's just that I need to get her on her own... or Dad... just one of them. I need to tell one of them what happened. I know they'll know what to do."

Tammy thought long and hard about

what Jake had told her.

"Dad told us that we should love our enemies because Jesus tells us to. I suppose Daniel is your enemy isn't he Jake?" Tammy waited for Jake to answer.

Jake nodded. "I suppose he is in a way. He is a bully."

"Do you have to forgive him then?" Tammy asked.

"I suppose I do," Jake said. "I don't know how though."

"You'd better ask God," suggested Tammy, "He's the one who said you have to do it."

Jake stopped and stared at Tammy. "How come you know all these things when you're only five years old?"

Tammy looked at Jake a little bit annoyed, "Five year olds aren't stupid you know! Perhaps I listen more than you do. You're always playing too much football!"

Jake didn't think that was true. He just thought that he had a smarty-pants for a little sister. Just then Jake heard the clatter and screech as the Euston Express drew into the station. Passengers spilled out onto the platform and a couple of minutes later

Jake spotted Mum and someone was with her. Daniel's train had arrived and he was coming this way.

When Daniel got in the car he didn't look at Jake or Tammy. He sat in the front seat with Mum and she talked to him as they drove out of the car park.

Jake felt sick in his stomach. Daniel made him feel so scared that he was actually feeling ill. Thankfully Daniel wasn't going to be with them for long. Joyce would be taking him back to her place when she was finished work.

That night when Jake was getting ready for bed, Mum looked in on Tammy and read her a bedtime story. Tammy asked Mum a question.

"What's a bully?"

"That's someone who is really nasty to someone just because they like to hurt them and see them cry."

"Why do they do it?"

"For lots of reasons. Sometimes hurting people makes them feel big and strong. Sometimes they don't have any friends. Sometimes things are going really badly at home..." Mum stopped and thought for a little. "Why are you asking me this Tammy?"

"Because Jake said that Daniel was

a bully and that he had thrown Jake's books in the puddle. Daniel is being nasty and Jake is scared."

Tammy could very rarely keep a secret, even when she tried hard. But this time she knew that somebody should tell Mum... so she did the right thing. Mum looked at Tammy and knew that she was telling the truth.

"That explains why Jake has been behaving strangely. He's been looking tired and worried. I'll talk to him and see what we can do. Well done Tammy for telling me. That's the best thing to do when someone is being bullied."

Mum then went next door to Jake's room to see how he was. He was in his pyjamas but wasn't in bed yet. Jake's gerbil, Chuckles, was running around the spinning red wheel in his cage and Jake was watching, quietly.

Mum came up to look at Chuckles too. "He's busy isn't he? It's funny how they always start waking up at this time of night. They get so energetic all of a sudden."

Jake nodded. Now might be a good time to tell about Daniel. Just then Dad came in too. Jake thought, it's definitely the right time. I'll tell both of them. But he just stood there, saying nothing.

Then Mum spoke up, "Have you something to tell your Dad and me Jake? You've not been yourself lately. Is anything wrong?"

Dad looked at Mum a bit puzzled. He didn't know yet what Tammy had told her a few minutes ago.

"Is it anything to do with Daniel?" Mum asked. "You didn't speak to him in the car and Tammy says that he threw your books in the puddle."

Jake then burst into tears. Dad came over and gave him a hug and they talked for quite a while about what had happened. Jake told them how he had hidden behind the hedge and what Daniel had done and how horrible it had made him feel.

It was late when Mum and Dad kissed Jake goodnight but as tomorrow was Sunday Jake was allowed a lie in. Jake couldn't believe it was a week since Daniel had started to bully him. Somehow it felt longer than that. Jake closed his eyes and drifted off to sleep. But not before he had thanked God. He looked at the stars twinkling above the oak tree that grew in their back garden. Jake whispered, "I'm in bed God, I'm just about to go to sleep... but thank you so much for helping me."

When Mr and Mrs MacDonald came back to check on him later all they heard was gentle snores. Jake was dreaming of swinging on the big tyre swing in the back garden on a lovely sunny day.

Joyce is a Help

The following day was Sunday. Before Jake came down to breakfast his mum and dad were sitting in the kitchen discussing Jake and Daniel's situation. Just as Jake was yawning and beginning to wake up they decided that they should both go and speak to Jake's headmaster. They prayed to God about what they should do and asked him to help them in the days ahead.

Jake woke up bright and breezy. He felt great. He brushed his teeth, washed his face and then rushed downstairs for some breakfast. Tammy looked a bit nervous at the breakfast table. She was worried that Jake would be angry with her for telling Mum. But Jake gave Tammy a big smile and even allowed her to have the last of the coco-pops. Tammy was really pleased that Jake was feeling happy once again.

At about 10 o'clock Dad gave Jake and Tammy a shout from the top of the stairs. "Get a move on you two. We leave for church in twenty minutes."

Tammy ran upstairs where Mum helped her brush her hair and change into her blue-flowery dress. Dad gulped down a last mouthful of tea and Jake changed his clothes. Everyone in the family looked quite smart as they got into the car to go to church.

As they arrived at the church door however, Jake got another surprise. He had forgotten about Daniel. Joyce was the Sunday school teacher at their church and Daniel had been staying with her. So of course, Daniel had come to church too. But now, even though Jake was still a bit scared of Daniel, he didn't feel quite as scared as before. He felt better now that he had spoken to his parents and to God about Daniel. The problem wasn't completely sorted but it was getting better.

Jake really enjoyed church. He loved the singing and the stories. It was really good to meet up with his friends too. Later on, in Sunday School, Jake ran up to Dave and whispered to him that he had told his mum all about it.

Dave patted Jake on the back and said, "Well done... and I see that Daniel's here this morning too?"

Jake nodded and said, "We still don't know why he's staying with Joyce, do we?"

Dave looked puzzled and shook his head. "You're right Jake. I can't work that one out at all. Maybe we'll find out more this morning. Joyce is asking us all to gather round. It looks as though she going to introduce Daniel."

Daniel was standing beside Joyce, looking dark and quiet. "He doesn't look very happy," thought Jake.

Then Joyce spoke up and said something very surprising.

"Hello boys and girls. I'd like to introduce you to a special friend of mine, Daniel. He is staying with me at the moment because I'm his auntie."

Jake's jaw dropped open in amazement. Daniel and Joyce were related. He couldn't believe it.

Joyce continued to speak. "Remember I told you about my sister who has been ill. Well Daniel's mum is my sister and she is in hospital for a few weeks but we hope she will be out soon. Daniel is missing her but Jake and Dave will look after him and make sure he knows what everyone's doing."

Jake and Dave both nodded. Jake was still a bit uncertain but Joyce was so nice - he'd do anything she asked.

Joyce then told everyone what they were going to do. "First of all we'll go into our groups and do our lessons. Then when everyone is finished we'll get together for a story and a game."

Daniel looked at Jake and didn't

smile, he didn't even try to look friendly. He just stared straight through Jake as though he was pretending that Jake didn't exist. Dave did his best and showed Daniel where he should sit. Soon everyone was either doing puzzles, crafts or helping make the big

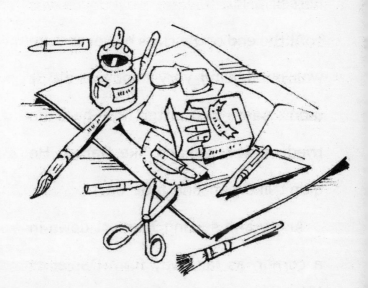

Sunday school poster which was going to be displayed in the church once it was finished.

Tammy was busy painting a big rainbow - she had been put in charge of the red stripe and was enjoying herself a lot.

At the end of the class however, Jake was not feeling very happy at all. It didn't seem to matter how hard he tried he still couldn't like Daniel. He didn't like him one little bit.

Angry and sulking Jake sat down in a corner, as far away from Daniel as he could get and when it was time for the story Jake didn't really feel in the mood for listening. Daniel was now sitting beside Dave and they were laughing together. That made Jake even angrier.

Tammy sat beside Jake and smiled at him. But Jake ignored her so she sat somewhere else. Then Joyce opened a big book with some pictures in it and began to tell the story.

'This is the story of the runaway son. There was once a boy who did something very stupid. He ran away from home. But before he ran away he asked his dad to give him lots of money. His dad loved the son so he gave him the money. But the son ran away and spent the lot. He wasted it.

Then one day he hadn't even enough money to buy any food and he realised how wicked and stupid he had been.

He decided then to go home and say sorry to his dad. When he got home he thought that he would ask his dad if he could become a family servant. Then he would have food to eat every day and some clothes to wear.

But what do you think happened?

When the runaway son got home his dad ran down the road to meet him. He was so glad that his son had come home he had a party to celebrate. He got lots of good food and even dressed his son in some expensive clothes and put a ring on his finger. But that's not the end of the story. The runaway son had an older brother. The older brother had never ran away, he had never wasted any money or disgraced his family like the other son had. But the older son felt very jealous of the attention that the younger son was getting.

The dad came out of the party to find the older son. He told him that they should all be happy that his brother had come home again. "It's just as if he was dead but now he has come back to life. Your brother was lost and now he is found.'"

Tammy raised her hand high in the air. "What is it Tammy?" asked Joyce.

"Did the older brother go back to the party then?"

Joyce smiled, "That's a good question, Tammy. What do you think he should have done?"

Tammy thought for a little and then said, "He should have gone in to the party. He was being a spoil sport."

Jake thought so too. The older brother should have made friends again with the runaway son. Jake couldn't stand people who were moody and sulky. "Am I being moody with Daniel?" he wondered. "I probably am."

Jake was confused. He had felt scared about being bullied by Daniel, he had felt angry about Daniel's new bike, then he had felt sorry about trying to throw it in the pond. But then Jake had felt relieved when he had spoken to his parents, and now here he was feeling angry all over again. "It's so hard to be good. And I still don't know what to do about Daniel. The problem just doesn't seem to go away.'

That night Jake spoke to his mum about it, while she was tucking him up in bed. She bent down to give him a kiss and then he asked her, "Mum, I don't like Daniel, but I feel sorry that his mum is in hospital. I suppose it was good that he came to Sunday

130

school. But I just don't like him. He was really horrible to me."

Mum looked worried and held Jake's hand. "It is difficult Jake. What Daniel did was wrong. He shouldn't have bullied you or made you frightened like that. But, he is having a hard time with his mum in hospital. However, we shouldn't just ignore this problem and hope that it goes away. You were right to tell us and we will speak to your headmaster about it tomorrow."

"But won't that make Daniel even angrier with me?" Jake was feeling scared again.

"If it does then it's Daniel's problem, not yours. If we tell the teachers about what has happened then they will help you and perhaps Daniel too.

"I know it is really difficult to like Daniel after what he has done to you. But Jesus Christ told us to love our enemies and to do good to people who have been nasty to us."

"Daniel's been very nasty to me."

"So what do you think you can do for Daniel that would be nice?"

Jake couldn't think.

"Sleep on it Jake. We might think of something in the morning."

As Jake yawned and closed his eyes he heard Dogger snuffling at the door to his room. Getting out of bed Jake went over to the door and opened it. "Hello boy, did you want a good night scratch behind your ears. Silly old dog." Jake carried on stroking the dog while trying to think of something he could do for Daniel. Dogger wagged his tail but wasn't much help at all. "Go to bed now Dogger," Jake sighed as he closed the door and got under the covers.

The Headmaster's Office

When Jake woke up the next morning he groaned. Mondays were always difficult. It was always harder to get organised after having had two whole days off school. Jake charged around looking for his soccer boots and then Dad hollered from the kitchen, "Come on Jake, we're going to have prayers now before you go to school."

Jake stopped what he was doing and ran down to the kitchen. The soccer boots would have to wait.

"We're going to read about King David today," Mum announced.

"David and Goliath?" asked Tammy.

"It's the same David, Tammy, but this story happened when he was a bit older. David had been chosen to be the next King of Israel instead of Saul. But for now Saul was still king and he didn't like David one bit. He was trying to capture him. Saul was jealous of David because the people liked him and he was a good soldier. One night

David and his men came across Saul sleeping in the back of a cave. David crept up to Saul without anybody noticing. In fact, David

was so close to Saul that he could have killed him easily, but he didn't. Instead he cut off a corner of Saul's coat and left Saul alone in the cave. David knew that it would have been wrong to kill Saul, so he didn't do it. Even though Saul had been trying to kill him."

Jake nodded, he understood what his mum was getting at.

"You see, God has given us rules to follow. Do you know what they are?"

Jake nodded, "The commandments."

"That's right. You can read about them in Exodus chapter 20. Do you see the notice I have pinned to the fridge with all the commandments written out on it?"

Tammy looked at the notice. She counted the numbers 1 through to 10. Then mum asked Jake, "Which command did David keep when he didn't kill King Saul."

"He kept number six, 'Do not kill.'"

"That's right. It would have been wrong of David to kill Saul. It would have displeased God, so he didn't do it. Sometimes we feel angry with people. We might not think about killing them but we feel the same way as somebody who wants to kill. Anger and hatred of other people is sinful."

Then Dad began to pray and everybody bowed their heads while he spoke to God.

"Dear God, thank you for loving us and caring for us. Thank you for the rules that you have given us to follow.

Help us to obey you. Help us to be like David, who when he was being bullied by Saul, still obeyed you and didn't kill Saul when he had the chance. Help us to love the people who hurt us and to do good to them instead of hurting them back. Thank you, Jesus, that when you were hurt and bullied by people you asked God to forgive them. You showed us how we should behave.

We hurt you too when we disobey you. But you loved us so much that you chose to die on the cross instead of us. Your love is amazing. Amen."

When Jake was being driven to

school that morning he felt amazed about how much Jesus loved him. "He died for me. He was willing to do it. He loves me so much." Going to school and facing up to Daniel didn't seem so bad now... now that he remembered that Jesus was with him always.

Jake felt a little nervous when they stood outside the headmaster's office. He wasn't sure what was going to happen. But it turned out alright. The headmaster spoke to Jake and his parents and asked Jake some questions. Jake told the headmaster exactly what had happened. He didn't make anything up or leave anything out. The headmaster then told Jake to go back to his class while he spoke to his mum and dad.

That night Mum served up cottage pie for tea. Jake was glad that she didn't cook green beans. He did not like green beans at all! Mum had also baked a cake for afters and Jake tucked into a slice as Dad spoke to him. "The headmaster will speak to Daniel and his dad tomorrow. I don't know what will happen, but if there's any more trouble you speak to a teacher and to us. Do you understand?"

"Yes Dad, I understand."

But there wasn't any trouble. Jake went to class, played in the school yard and went home at 4 o'clock and Daniel didn't bother him one bit.

Jake felt as if everything had now worked out fine. "Daniel isn't going to bother me any more. I can just ignore him and he can just ignore me. That will be perfect." Jake thought.

The Bible story the next morning was about Peter. "Do you remember what happened to Jesus before he died?"

"People hurt him," burst out Tammy.

"Yes, and something else. Do you remember what his friends did?"

Tammy and Jake weren't sure.

"Well, in the Bible it tells us 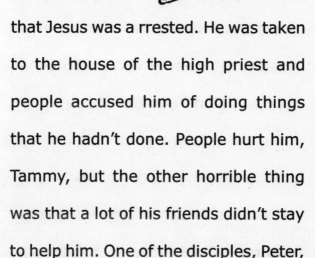 that Jesus was a rrested. He was taken to the house of the high priest and people accused him of doing things that he hadn't done. People hurt him, Tammy, but the other horrible thing was that a lot of his friends didn't stay to help him. One of the disciples, Peter, said that he didn't know him. Three times he denied that he knew Jesus. And then they took Jesus away to kill him."

Jake knew a little about what that was like. Though none of his friends had treated him as bad as Jesus' friends had... Jake still felt horrible about how he hadn't heard from Timothy. It was as if his friend had left him behind and didn't care at all.

But then Jake rememberd that he hadn't written Timothy either.

"Perhaps he is waiting for a letter from me?" Jake thought. And then he felt guilty. He'd let his bad feelings stop him getting in touch with Timothy. He'd thought about asking for Timothy's address but then he'd gone into a sulk and hadn't done anything about it. "Life will be really busy for Timothy. He won't have time to write letters. I'll get his address tomorrow."

This made Jake feel better. Instead of being gloomy about Timothy he was happy and cheerful. He was going to do something instead of sulking.

Dad was still talking about the story so Jake focused again on what he was saying. Dad asked another question,

"What happened after they killed Jesus?"

Jake knew the answer to this one, "Jesus came back to life again."

"That's right Jake. And one of the people he saw when he came back to life was Peter. Peter was sorry about what he had done and Jesus forgave him. Peter had been one of Jesus' close friends and he had not been with him when it mattered. It was a horrible thing for Peter to do. But Jesus showed how good and loving he was by forgiving Peter. Jesus also forgives us for the sins we do.

"Often we think about the horrible way others treat us, but we forget about the horrible way we treat God. It is because of us that Jesus had to die on the cross. So just as Jesus forgives us we should forgive others."

All of a sudden the phone rang and mum dashed to pick it up. The ringing stopped and Jake heard mum's voice speaking down the phone. "No, Joyce, no, we understand that Daniel's been through a lot. There was nothing you could do. Daniel will settle down now that he is getting the support he needs from you and from the school."

Jake listened harder but just then mum said goodbye. Then she hung up.

Just then the phone rang again. Mum sighed and said something about the phone always ringing when she was busy. But when she lifted the phone her voice was much more cheerful. "Timothy! How good to hear from you. How are your parents? Really? Well… hang on a second. I'll go and get Jake."

But before she could even turn the door knob Jake was in the sitting room, taking the phone off her and almost shouting down the phone.

"Timothy, how are you? I've missed you. How's your new school. Are you still rubbish at maths?"

Jake and Timothy had a long talk. Timothy explained how they had spent the summer with their grandmother in the North. "Then Gran got sick and Mum and Dad had to look after her. Dad heard there was a job available in the company offices up here. It turned out that he could start immediately. So we're all at Gran's now. Me and my brother are in new schools now.

Everything is really busy. I'm sorry that I didn't write."

"That's all right," Jake laughed. "I didn't write either. But I'll send you a letter next week."

Timothy laughed next, "There's no need. Next weekend I'm coming to stay with my Auntie Paula - on the next street to you. She's been helping with Gran and is going to give me a lift down after school on Friday night."

Jake was so excited he felt he was going to burst any second.

"I've got an even better idea. Come and stay over at my place. We've got sleeping bags and camp beds. We could put one up on my bedroom floor. I'll ask Mum..." Jake took a deep breath and hollered, "MUM!"

"There's no need to shout Jake. I heard you, and yes, Timothy can stay over, if his mum agrees."

Jake and Timothy both cheered.

The next day Jake was up very early. He was excited about Timothy's visit and he felt great. All the bad feelings about Daniel and the bullying had gone away. Once breakfast was finished, he got ready to walk into school.

"Remember your spelling book." she

 called out. "You left it on the settee. And don't go so fast, remember you're walking Tammy to school today. Tammy are you ready?" Tammy yelled "Yes," from somewhere upstairs and Jake grinned. The excitement of school still hadn't worn off. Tammy was as keen as she had been on the very first day.

As he waited for Tammy Jake's Mum decided to have a little chat about Daniel. "You know that Daniel has had a hard time..." Jake nodded. "What he did was wrong and you had a horrible time, but it might be good to show Daniel that you've forgiven him. You and Daniel and Timothy could do something together. Dave Johnson could join in too. All four of you could sleep over next weekend. I'll leave it up to you. If you ask them just tell me and I'll get things organised."

Jake wasn't so sure about that idea. He had wanted to have Timothy to himself. He didn't want to share his best friend with anyone.

Tammy jumped down the last three steps and stood smartly for inspection. "Your skirt is a bit squint Tammy, let me straighten it. There now. You're ready." Mum gave Jake and Tammy a hug before they went out the door.

She whispered to Jake, "Remember how Jesus has forgiven you. You should show the same forgiveness to others."

"But what if Daniel bullies me again?" Jake asked.

"If he bullies you again tell me straight away. But Joyce thinks that Daniel has changed now that he has spoken about his feelings. He is going to get help and we should be willing to help him too."

Jake waved goodbye to his mum at

the door and made his way along the road to school. Tammy skipped along quietly at first and then she yelled out loudly, "Hi Daniel. Are you ready to go to school?"

Jake groaned quietly. He had been secretly hoping that they would walk past Daniel's house without him noticing. "No chance of that now," Jake grumbled. Daniel had been bent over the wheel of the dark-blue bike. Now he was staring at Tammy and Jake coming down the street. Just then Jake noticed that Daniel was struggling to get air into a flat tyre. Jake felt like laughing and then he realised it would be wrong. "God wants me to forgive Daniel and to do something good for him."

So Jake knelt beside Daniel while Tammy practised doing balancing on the edge of the pavement.

"Can I give you a hand Daniel?" Jake asked anxiously. "I can hold the bike while you put the air in the tyre."

Daniel didn't look up. He just kept staring at the bike tyre. Jake continued to speak, "It's a lovely bike, really cool."

Daniel stopped what he was doing and looked up. Jake remembered what his mum had said. Should I ask him to come to the sleep-over or not? Daniel would like it. Timothy wouldn't mind. Jake carried on speaking, "Hawthorn wood is a good place to go cycling."

Daniel nodded, "There are good tracks there. I cycle there quite a bit." Daniel and Jake stared at each other. It was strange that they were both having a conversation. Jake knew that if he didn't ask Daniel to the sleep-over now he never would.

What do you think Jake will do? Will he ask Daniel to come to the sleep-over or will he just forget about it? What would you do?

Jake and Daniel: If Jake remembers God's instructions to love our enemies then the two boys might get on quite well. There are people we get on best with and others who we just like. There are different types of relationships and if we follow God's rules then these friendships will be easier. People will always have problems with each other because people are sinners and can be nasty and hurt other people. This is wrong but God will listen to you when you tell him you are sorry. He will forgive you when you ask him. We can ask God to help us love others as much as we love ourselves.

Jesus and me: Jesus understands about being bullied. He was bullied by people who wanted to kill him. Some of his friends even pretended that they didn't know him at all. Even people in Jesus' family didn't stick up for him. Jesus understands about being sad and lonely. He is a good person to talk to about it. But always, always, talk to a parent, teacher or other responsible grown up. God has given you family members, teachers and friends for a reason. He can use them to help you. Bullying is not something you should keep a secret. Tell someone about it. We all have problems that we need to share.

Stories from Canterbury Place

The other title in this series:
The Big Green Tree at No. 11
Tammy and Jake learn about
Life and Death.
ISBN: 1-85792-731-1

CHRISTIAN FOCUS

Staying faithful – Reaching out!

Christian Focus Publications publishes books for adults and children under its three main imprints: Christian Focus; Mentor and Christian Heritage. Our books reflect that God's word is reliable and Jesus is the way to know him, and live forever with him.

Our children's publication list includes a Sunday school curriculum that covers pre-school to early teens; puzzle and activity books. We also publish personal and family devotional titles, biographies and inspirational stories that children will love.

If you are looking for quality Bible teaching for children then we have an excellent range of Bible story and age specific theological books.

From pre-school to teenage fiction, we have it covered!

Find us at our web page:
www.christianfocus.com